PIERO VENTURA

CLOTHING

Garments, Styles, and Uses

With the Collaboration of
Max Casalini
Laura Battaglia
Marisa Murgo Ventura
Antonella Toffolo

HOUGHTON MIFFLIN COMPANY

BOSTON 1993

CONTENTS

Copyright © 1992 by Arnoldo Mondadori Editore S.p.A.
English translation © 1993 Arnoldo Mondadori Editore S.p.A.
First American edition 1993
Originally published in Italy in 1992 by Mondadori
All rights reserved. For information about permission
to reproduce selections from this book, write to
Permissions, Houghton Mifflin Company,
215 Park Avenue South, New York, New York 10003.
Cataloging-in-Publication Data is available from the U.S. Library of Congress.
Printed in Italy by Arnoldo Mondadori - Verona
10 9 8 7 6 5 4 3 2 1

INTRODUCTION

Why do we wear clothes? Do we wear them to protect ourselves from hot and cold weather, or do we just want to display ourselves, to be admired, to demonstrate that we are wealthy enough to buy expensive and fashionable things? It's easy to see that both reasons are true. Clothes are the product of two different needs. First, when we have used clothes to cover ourselves, they have always done the job. Looking at this aspect, we can reconstruct a "technical history" of clothes, how they were produced in different ages, of what materials they were made, and especially, with what kinds of fabrics. Second, where clothes are a symbol of prestige, we can trace a history of fashion, of the meanings that little by little have been associated with different garments, and of course the people who wore them.

The first clothes were rough smocks made from animal skins sewn together with strips, also made either from skins or perhaps animal tendons. Later with farming and agriculture, people began to use plant fibers like linen and hemp and animal fleece like that of goats and sheep to make threads. If you laid out parallel threads (the warp) and weaved in a series of perpendicular threads (called the weft or woof) you would end up with a fabric. People even learned how to make rather crude but warm and practical material simply by pressing together wool fibers (known as felt). The filament from a caterpillar, patiently unwound from its cocoon, could become a precious yarn—silk—and a liquid taken from a mollusc's bladder could be used as a wool dye (purple). Later other natural dyes were used, and today we can create completely artificial materials like acetates and acrylic yarns.

People have always tried to use fashions to emphasize certain features of the body that they found interesting—men's large shoulders and women's "waspish" waists, for example. Even the quality of materials has been loaded with conventional and symbolic meanings—silk is sophisticated, hemp is simple and rough, wool is soft and warm. The story of purple is a good example of this; it went from being a prestigious fabric for the rich symbolizing the power of imperial Rome where only the emperor could wear it (hence the phrase "born to the purple"), to being a symbol of religious authority in the vestments of cardinals in the Christian Church.

An examination of people's clothing through the ages is not just an entertaining exercise. It allows us to go over the important stages of history and perhaps even helps us to understand not only how our ancestors wanted to be seen, but also how they wanted to see themselves.

PREHISTORY

Prehistoric Europe was certainly a hostile place for those first representatives of *Homo sapiens sapiens* who, appearing at the end of the Paleolithic Age, tried to survive there. It was the time of the last Ice Age, when enormous frozen expanses covered the northern regions. There was no snow and dangerous animals lurked in dense forests.

In this cold and threatening world, people learned to hunt, fish, gather fruit from trees, and protect themselves from the bitter weather. The first garments were of course the skins of the large animals that were hunted for food: mammoths, bears, bison, and reindeer. At first the skins were thrown over the shoulder and tied around the body for casual protection, but then people learned how to make tools out of the bones, teeth, and horns of these animals.

So they made needles out of ivory tusks and used tendons as thread to sew furs together for more practical garments. They made knives and scrapers out of bone and horn to cut and clean animal skins better. And once people had what they needed, they also thought of making what they liked; prehistoric settlements often contain minutely decorated necklace beads made of animal teeth or bone. They were probably magic symbols, or amulets, but they also demonstrate creative inspiration, a search for beauty, and, who knows, maybe even a bit of flirting!

Fire provided warmth, kept animals away, and cooked meat, but soon people noticed that it was also useful for smoking skins to help preserve them.

Hunting and fishing were the main sources of food for prehistoric nomadic tribes.

Large flat stones, crossed with furrows and lines, prove that once the skins were cleaned, they were cut with flint knives and then probably sewn.

The nemeth, a cloth that was arranged around the head, was a typical headdress.

EGYPT

The hot climate had a lot to do with fashion in ancient Egypt, and in fact at the beginning of their civilization Egyptians wore a simple loincloth that was the same for everyone. The only distinction between high-ranking officials and the populace was the kind of material used; finest linen was worn by the pharaoh and the upper classes, whereas ordinary men and soldiers wore leather and woven material. They often wore one or more transparent skirts of differing lengths over the loincloth, held at the waist by a belt.

Women's fashion was more refined, partly because women in Egyptian society were always respected and honored. They wore a long transparent tunic over the same loincloth men wore; called a kalasiris, it came up to below the breast and was held up by colored belts and shoulder straps that crossed over in front of or delicately veiled the breasts.

Clothing, however, was considered an ornament; used in the home to look elegant, garments were quickly cast off if people needed freedom of movement. This habit of walking around naked also fostered a great deal of care for the body, which always had to be smooth, hairless, and scrupulously clean.

Shoes were uncommon; only kings, officials, and priests wore simple sandals during ceremonies.

Hair, both real and in wigs, was arranged in braids or curls.

Jewels such as necklaces, bracelets, and anklets were usually gold, but the Egyptians also used majolica and glass to make jeweled necklaces that looked like collars or belts of multicolored beads.

The Egyptians used thin, lightweight materials and dyed them many colors, each with a symbolic meaning: white was associated with happiness, as was blue, which was considered symbolic of the skin of Ammon, god of the air; green symbolized life and youth; and golden yellow stood for the skin of the gods.

When skirts were short, they had a triangular or trapezoidal shape. The high priest wore a leopard skin over his pleated skirt as a sign of distinction.

To avoid getting sunburn or insect bites, people daily rubbed perfumed oils into their skin.

At first used to protect people from the sun, wigs soon became a very important accessory for both men and women; they could be of different colors and even gilded.

Frescoes and bas-reliefs indicate the surprising fact that over the many thousands of years of Egyptian culture only small changes took place in clothing and these happened very slowly. Even makeup, a very important part of female beauty, had fixed rules: the face was covered with foundation and the cheekbones were emphasized by a yellow-red paste placed high and smeared toward the temples. Lips were drawn with a brush, using the same paste as on the cheeks. The most attention was paid to the eyes; the eyelids were tinged green, above and below, and smeared toward the eyebrows with a dark gray powder. The final touch was black kohl, still used today by Bedouin women, which outlined the eyes, making them look bigger and longer.

The most ancient garment was a skirt made of sheepskin.

Rich people's kandys went down to the ankles and was decorated with fringes and embroidery; soldiers and peasants wore a short simple one.

A polos was a headdress often pictured worn by Phoenician goddesses.

THE ANCIENT EAST

Four thousand years before Christ, in the plain between the Tigris and Euphrates rivers, a sophisticated and wealthy civilization developed at the same time as ancient Egypt. That corner of the earth where this civilization grew was called Mesopotamia, which means "between the rivers," because it lay between the two bodies of water that made the earth there very fertile. The community that developed was therefore based on agriculture, but soon the society divided into more complex systems, and over the centuries different groups became powerful: the Sumerians, the Babylonians, and the Assyrians.

In the Middle East of ancient times there were also other civilizations: the Hittites of the Anatolian mountains, the Persians, and the Phoenicians, whose commercial activity on the sea made them more of a maritime power than a state with definite boundaries.

Different peoples then, but with many things in common that allowed them to have similar viewpoints. In the beginning, society's agricultural activity brought about a very simple way of dressing in sheepskins, probably with fringes, worn at the waist like a skirt. After this primitive Sumerian garment came the adoption of textiles and the habit of draping oneself with floor-length robes hung over the left shoulder and arm and leaving the right shoulder free. This robe developed into a rich fringed drape, called a kaunace, made of precious wool, which was wrapped in a spiral around the body. The kaunace was worn over the tunic, called a kandys, which was a typical garment first of the Assyrian-Babylonians, then of the Persians. The kandys was of various lengths, was sewn with sleeves as well, could be made of linen, silk, or cotton, and was embroidered, brightly colored, or decorated with fringes, depending on the importance of the wearer.

Phoenician women wore their hair divided into ornate braids, or bound in cloth strips like a turban. Tight, colorful skirts were common, fixed under the bosom.

Persians commonly wore soft cloth trousers, called anaxyrides. On top they wore a short kandys and a cloak that could have had a fur edge.

The Phoenicians traded many cloths and dyes; most popular were blue, yellow, all shades of red, and especially purple, over which they had a monopoly.

Assyrians took care of their hair and beards, which they grew long and curly, perfumed with oils, and even bound with gold threads. On their forehead they had a cloth or a rounded metal tiara to keep their hair back, but the king wore a different kind of tiara, which was blue and white and had ribbons (or infulae) that fell to his shoulders.

After being skinned, the hide was cleaned and scraped while resting against a tree trunk; this was the ancestor of the more recent cambered bench.

In Paleolithic times, sewing was done by making holes along the edges of the hide with a point of flint and then winding with tendons or laces.

The Greeks and Romans used leather a lot, but it was only during the conquest of Britain at the time of Caesar that the Romans saw leather used for making clothes and holding up the barbarians' breeches.

Leather could also be worked until it became as soft as fabric, so that it could be sewn with finer needles to make light women's clothes.

TANNING LEATHER

The discovery of bone scrapers used to clean animal skins has shown that leather was used even in Paleolithic times, but we don't know exactly when people learned how to make soft leather out of hard animal hide.

One of the main problems was tanning, the process that stops skins from decomposing; of the many systems that must have been tried one of the first to work was the use of fat, rubbed into the skin with specially made tools while many people held the hide taut. Later, for this kind of tanning, oil was used.

Another process was the use of alum; many discoveries point to its common use among the Egyptians. Hides tanned with alum turn white and harden, a fact that favored its use in making shoes, and only after further treatments could it be softened. Furthermore, the white color was used when

The first systems of preserving leather were fumigation and desiccation, which was done by laying the skins out to dry or spreading salt on them.

dyeing the leather yellow, green, or blue.

A third system used the tannic acid contained in oak tree bark and gall (the spherical excretion that forms on leaves after certain insects leave their eggs there). This technique was definitely know to the Hittites and Babylonians, because we know of large oak groves planted for this purpose.

Tanning with oil, alum, and vegetable substances was, even after developments, still in use in the nineteenth century. The choice of treatments was determined by the color that each process gave to the leather. Oil tanning turned leather brown, alum tanning left the leather white, and vegetable tanning colored the leather all shades of beige and reddish brown.

The first leather clothes appeared in Paleolithic times and show traces of sewing. Containers were also made of leather, and within the time of written records, there were many different kinds of bags for carrying water, grain, and even women's personal objects. In Egypt sandals, cushions, and clothes were often dyed red and sewn with threads decorated with glass beads. Again in Egypt there is even the documented use of leather gloves.

Among the Babylonians, leather preparation in the form of goatskin footwear reached a high level of artistic craftsmanship. These shoes were colored and decorated with jewels and embroidery. The quality of the goatskin, which in Babylon was typically dyed red, became so famous that even Roman emperors wore Babylonian red leather shoes.

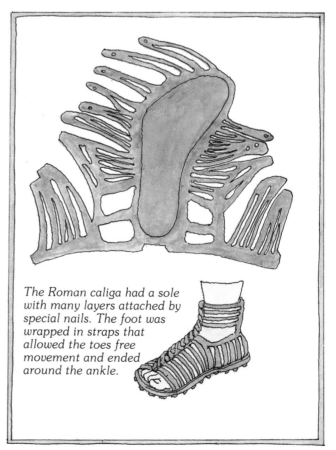

The Roman caliga had a sole with many layers attached by special nails. The foot was wrapped in straps that allowed the toes free movement and ended around the ankle.

Men and women shaved themselves carefully and bathed every day.

Hats of different shapes were very common and were attached to the hair with large gold pins.

Clothes were made more precious by using sophisticated materials, dyed with sought-after colors and woven with gold and silver threads.

CRETE: A HAPPY ISLAND

Seventeen hundred years before Christ, on an island in the middle of the Mediterranean Sea, a civilization flourished renowned for its wealth and culture; it was the civilization of Crete. Nurtured by the sun and fine weather, and taking advantage of their island's advantageous position at the center of the sea-faring commerce of the time, the Cretans led a lively and enjoyable social life. They were cultured and loved beautiful things, which we know from the frescoes found in the island's palaces.

Elegant athletes, their naked bodies anointed with perfumed oils, whirled around the pointed horns of bulls; they were completely naked, because any fabric could have presented a dangerous obstacle in their exercises. When they finished bullfighting, the young wore loincloths with a piece of material hanging over the front, sometimes decorated with beads. They tied other leather belts around the waist to make shoulders and chests look more impressive, and they wore well-made boots or light shoes

on their feet. In the winter they wore shawls of wool or fur, which were sometimes waterproofed with oil or covered with leather tiles, and the loincloth could become a short triangular skirt, shorts, or wide, knee-length trousers.

Women's fashions were just as precious and detailed. The Cretan woman had a very important role in society, and this explains the constant search for originality and sophistication in women's clothes. High-ranking women wore long skirts, often with different-colored overlapping layers and a tight-fitting bodice that was tied under the breasts and had elbow-length sleeves. The waist was emphasized by a belt. On top of the skirt they wore a small apron embroidered at the front and the back.

Ordinary women wore simple rough linen tunics, which went down to the ankle and were tied by a leather belt, just like men who had knee-length tunics.

The imaginative Cretan fashion was the exception in ancient times, considering that in the centuries that followed austere Greek styles prevailed, which were baggy and draped.

Colors used in clothing were bold and contrasting; red, light blue, yellow, black, and purple were mixed daringly to produce new and vivacious effects.

Skirts were wide or narrow, flounced, and could be decorated with very small gold plates sewn on to form animal or plant designs.

Elegant women had long hair, which hung down or was bound in a ponytail with ribbons or with bone and metal hairpins or gathered in hair nets.

When the material of a chiton was particularly rich, it was draped to form false sleeves; the tunic was then called a keridos.

Women already wore bras, which were a band of material called a strophium, and they used tight bandages to make themselves look thinner.

There was also the custom of sewing small oval weights in the hem of a peplos to keep the material closer to the body.

Women had long hair, but there were many different hairstyles. Spartan women, for example, cut their hair short in the front and gathered the rest in a ponytail. Buns were common too, gathered in a little bag or in straps that framed the face.

A beard could have different shapes; after Alexander the Great, however, men usually shaved themselves completely so as not to be grabbed by the beard in battle.

Blond hair was so sought after that men and women tried various methods to lighten their hair like washing it in lye or drying it in the sun.

There were different kinds of hats: a very high conical Egyptian hat, a pagoda shape imported from the east, or the Phrygian cap. The pilos was common, a cap without a brim that was also worn under a helmet, and a petasos, a large-brimmed felt hat.

After Alexander the Great's campaigns in the east, silk and cotton arrived in Greece and were used to make very light materials. Embroidery also became popular, but patterns remained typically Greek: spirals, oblongs, and zigzags.

In Greek times the use of cotton and silk made cloaks light and airy, and delicate colors like pink cyclamen and pastel green were preferred, as well as all shades of gold.

A himation could also be worn on its own, on top of a simple loincloth; in fact the Greeks spent most of their time outdoors, and for this reason they preferred wide comfortable garments, which could be taken off quickly.

GREEK STYLE

The Hellenic society that spread throughout the Mediterranean Sea one thousand years before Christ was originally pastoral and austere, and the accumulated wealth did not change the simplicity of Greek style; the chiton, the himation, the chlamys, and the peplos were the few garments used.

The chiton was a simple tunic of differing lengths, which was worn by both men and women and could be clasped at the left shoulder or on both shoulders by metal buckles.

With the passing of time and an increase in wealth, the draping of the chiton became more frivolous, especially when worn by women; the close-fitting austere woolen garment was made of richer material and was adorned with so many pleats and flaps that it

became a peplos, a typical Greek woman's garment. Now the peplos was a long cloth rectangle, sewn on one side or just drawn close, that hung from the shoulders where it was folded so as to fall over the chest. Two shoulder buckles held the front and back together, while only one leather belt was worn tight around the waist or under the breasts to gather the material and emphasize the shape of the body.

The himation was a wide rectangular material used like a cloak or, doubled up, like a short and heavy cloak for protecting the shoulders and head. The chlamys was a short cloak, used mainly by Athenian youths and soldiers, that was fastened by a shoulder buckle.

Although the chiton and himation were white at first, later they were dyed red, purple, violet, yellow, and turquoise.

Hats were not used often, except by travelers, who wore wide-brimmed head coverings. A traveling stick was also common, as well as the use of solid shoes.

A woman's working garment was a simple sleeveless tunic that was usually worn under the stola.

The toga was the most symbolic garment in Roman society, representing the free citizen; it was made of a long, wide band of white wool which was draped over the right shoulder and arm, leaving the left arm free.

Breeches, which were of barbarian origin, became common mostly among travelers and people who worked out in the open.

Even upper-class women spun, wove, and made their own clothes.

ROME

In the Roman Republic men and women wore simple garments that consisted of pieces of wool or linen cloth; cotton and silk were very expensive because they had to be imported from the east. These pieces of material were not very wide, because they were home-made on vertical looms, which limited their size. Only later, thanks to new techniques for making the frames of looms, were fabrics made wider so as to drape with richer folds.

The most ancient garment was a simple cloak called a trabea, made by folding a piece of cloth and placing it on one or both shoulders. Ordinary people often wore it with a tunic similar to the Greek chiton. Women wore a sleeveless tunic, almost like a petticoat, and matrons wore another bigger and richer tunic called a stola on top of that.

17

CLASSICAL SOCIETY

In a complex and diverse society like that of the Romans, garments eventually became a way of classifying and recognizing the social class of the person wearing them, more than they had ever been in the past. The best example of this is the toga, which was reserved exclusively for Roman citizens and could not be worn by foreigners, slaves, or freedmen.

Even the color changed according to the person who was wearing the toga; if it was white, or bleached–*candidatus* in Latin–then the person was a public official (this is where the term *candidate* for people who want to be elected to public duties comes from); a brown toga was worn as a sign of mourning; a toga praetexta had a purple stripe and was worn only by citizens' sons who were not yet of age, by magistrates, senators, priests, and knights: the size of the purple stripe indicated which category the person was in. The toga picta, or palmata, was purple with embroidered gold and silver palm trees or stars and was worn by generals in a triumph, their official parade. And finally there was the toga virilis, which was made of white wool and worn by Roman citizens after their sixteenth birthday, when they officially became adults.

There were also several cloaks worn by different social classes; the pallium was a square cloak that was hung on the left shoulder instead of a toga and was worn by scholars

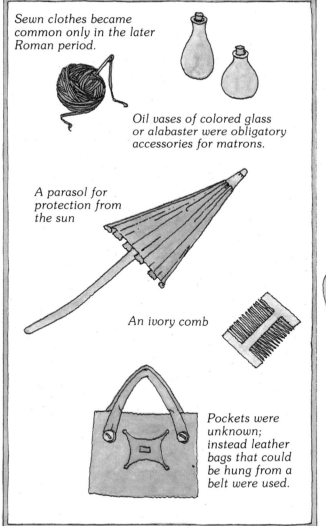

Sewn clothes became common only in the later Roman period.

Oil vases of colored glass or alabaster were obligatory accessories for matrons.

A parasol for protection from the sun

An ivory comb

Pockets were unknown; instead leather bags that could be hung from a belt were used.

Charioteers wore short tunics and strips of braided leather to protect their chest. Their head covering was also made of leather.

An elegant matron of imperial Rome

18

Patricians and knights

The middle class: the free and freed slaves

| Standard-bearer | Peasant woman | Gladiator | Actor | Dancer | Innkeeper's wife |

and senators; the chlamys was Greek, used often among soldiers and hung from the right shoulder. A paludamentum was a purple cloak worn by generals; and finally there was the humble trabea, which with the passing of centuries became a large decorated cloak worn by emperors, consuls, and knights.

The lacerna, a cloak used to shield from rain, often had a hood (called a cucullus) and was common among patricians and soldiers. Servants had a paenula, a short tunic, which was covered by a cloak called a sagum, a small square piece of cloth with a hole to let the head through.

Rich matrons wore a large cloak, a palla, over the stola which they used to cover their heads when they went out. People liked tassels and embroidered designs depicting objects in nature or shapes. Favorite colors were light blue, yellow, red, light green, and pink.

Typical of the upper classes was the love of hairstyles; though men had short hair and shaven faces, women had complicated and sophisticated hairdos, dyed their hair, and curled it in a tight mass around the face or allowed it to escape from ribbons in wild curls. The rules of fashion in this respect were varied and so clearly set out through the ages that even today those hairstyles are used to date accurately statues, vases, and frescoes.

Even footwear could show the class of the wearer; senators wore black shoes, patricians wore red shoes decorated with buckles and studs, and rich matrons liked red or gold shoes decorated with ornaments and precious stones. Buskins, shoes with high wooden soles, were popular and were also worn by actors.

Precious and delicately made pins and belts were used to clasp the cloak over the shoulder and to gather the tunic at the waist.

A tablion was a precious cloth panel attached to the chlamys of dignitaries.

Often anaxyrides were tucked into leggings.

Tunics had richly decorated tight sleeves.

A typical Oriental dress was a round-cut cloak, a short tunic with decorated borders, and tight-fitting breeches called anaxyrides.

Priests wore a dalmatic, which was later adopted by civilians.

Women wore a veil over their heads which fell along the back and was sometimes clasped by a pear-and-jewel circlet.

The empress wore a wide and long cloak like the one worn by men. A maniakion, a collar made of precious material and jewels, was also common.

Women had long hair and gathered it in bunches tied with ribbons or held by a net decorated with gems called a calantica.

THE IMPERIAL CITY OF BYZANTIUM

The imperial court at Byzantium was the political and cultural heir to the greatness of Rome, but the Oriental love of magnificence led to a lot of changes in dress styles. Although garments there had evolved from Greece and Rome, they became more linear, no longer softly draped around the body, but rigidly vertical to give a greater sense of power and majesty. Wool and linen were still common, but among the upper classes richly decorated, damasked fabrics became popular. Rulers had the privilege of wearing silk produced in the court from grubs imported from the east in the sixth century.

Men usually wore a short tunic, tied by a belt, and tight-fitting leggings. The emperor and his dignitaries wore a long chlamys over the tunic, derived from the Roman version, which was decorated at the front with an embroidered and jeweled panel of cloth called a tablion.

A loron was also a symbol of power; it consisted of a long sash of damasked silk, lined with precious fabric and enriched with gold and precious stones, that could be of differing lengths but was usually about fifteen to twenty centimeters wide and worn over the tunic.

Women wore a tight-sleeved tunic, on top of which they wore another, which hung to the ground and was very decorative, called Byzantine. Richly embroidered and even embossed fabrics were used, with designs taken from both nature and geometry, such as orbs (common circular shapes).

Soft leather shoes, or a campagus of silk with a sole, were black when reserved for dignitaries, and purple or gold decorated with gold buckles and precious stones for the emperor.

Over their short tunics and rough cloth jackets barbarians wore furs to protect them from the harsh climate.

In addition to furs, men could wear a small square or rectangular cloak of rough cloth or leather, which was gathered at the chest by metal clasps, some of which were quite elaborate. Breeches were often of goatskin.

Despite the collapse of the Roman Empire and the destruction of many of its monuments, the barbarians could not resist the charm of such a splendid culture and were influenced by it in many areas, with very original results.

Women wore a short shirt tucked into their skirt, but later the shirt became as long as an entire dress.

Warriors wore bronze or bronze-and-leather helmets. In more northern countries the practice of decorating the helmet with animal horns or shaping the bronze to imitate horns was very common.

THE BARBARIANS

The barbarians were, generally speaking, the peoples that lived on the northern edge of the Roman Empire who, when it collapsed, invaded, sacked, and pillaged everywhere. We are therefore talking about many different peoples with different cultures but, from a Roman point of view, with more similarities than differences.

Barbarians were mostly nomadic tribes where tall, strong men wore flowing beards and mustaches to symbolize their status as freemen. Clothing was simple and appropriate for the cold northern climate, but there was a surprising feature: the barbarians were already cutting fabric when the Romans were still limited to draping entire pieces of material around their bodies. These men of the north wore a fabric tunic cut to let head and arms through, and usually made of wool, hemp, or linen. On top of this short rectangular shirt, men wore a leather tunic, while their legs were covered by long trousers that ended inside leather boots.

Women wore a tunic similar to the men's, but theirs was ankle-length and covered with a cloak.

Once they came into contact with Rome and Byzantium, these peoples adopted more comfortable and pleasant clothing; they started to use sleeves and finer fabrics and added decorative trimmings. There was also the widespread manufacture of jewels that were always colorful thanks to the glazes or enamels used with many-colored stones.

FROM SHEEP TO CLOTH

Although practiced since ancient times, the Greeks and Romans perfected wool weaving with excellent results. It was then, in fact, that a demand was growing for softer and finer fabrics, and for this reason breeds of sheep with the best fleece were selected. They even produced a kind of wool called *pellitum*, which means "covered," because while the fleece was growing it was protected with skins to keep it from being ruined.

After the sheep were shorn, the wool was selected, washed, and carded or combed. Combing divided the wool into long, parallel fibers that were then twisted into a tight, shiny yarn.

After being carded or combed, the wool was spun; the tools most used for this purpose up to the fifteenth century were a distaff and spindle. The spun yarn was then woven on a loom, and the cloth produced was fulled, that is, soaked with certain substances such as human urine, plant ashes, or a soapy solution, and then beaten to thicken the fibers and hide the weave.

The last step in the process was dyeing the wool; this was done by soaking the cloth in vegetable or animal coloring. The procedure was different if you wanted to bleach the wool, in which case it was exposed to sulfurous vapors.

Fibers wound around a distaff were then twisted and rewound around the spindle. A long distaff could be inserted in a belt. leaving the hands free.

Already in classical times, instead of cards, people used crude tools made for carding wool.

It seems that shearers for shaving animals didn't appear until Roman times. Until then the fleece was pulled out by hand.

The first tools built especially for carding wool were made in the Middle Ages; they were small planks of wood partly covered in leather from which a series of angled metal points protruded.

A series of vertical threads, called a warp, were arranged on a loom, and then another thread was passed through them lengthwise, forming the woof.

The oldest looms were vertical and people wove standing up. Gradually, the structure changed until it became a horizontal loom, which first appeared in Europe in medieval times and whose origins are unknown.

Red was a difficult dye to make in ancient times because it quickly turned pink. One of the most common dyes was obtained from an insect called cochineal, called kermes by the Arabs, which is where the words carmine and crimson come from.

25

A PYRAMIDAL SOCIETY

The barbarian tribes that settled along the borders of the Roman Empire were nomads, and they did not know the comfort of brick houses or the splendor of silk. Attracted by the wonders on the other side of the fence, they started to creep in, until in the fifth century they turned into a cyclone and destroyed everything.

Roman Europe fell into chaos, and for five hundred years there was no peace. Cities were abandoned, crafts were forgotten, roads and bridges crumbled, and commerce died out. Silk became just a memory, and sophisticated and colorful fabrics disappeared along with basic commodities. Fear controlled people's lives and induced them to ask for protection from powerful warriors who had constructed well-defended castles, or from monasteries, which did not have soldiers but did have thick walls to hide behind.

Life was hard, and the last thing people thought about was clothing. Clothes were made at home and were dingy, rough, and shapeless. Trousers protected legs from the

King

Pope

Feudal lords

High clerics

Vassals   Vavasor   Vavasory

Clerics

Peasants and serfs

The few roads that still existed were in a bad state, bridges were scarce, and brigands were common. For this reason during the Dark Ages, which lasted until about 1000, populations were tightly bound to the land surrounding the feudal lord's castle. People moved around only when there were festivals in other cities. These were the only occasions on which people could buy or look at different goods and have a chance to sell their own food or objects and fabrics made for sale.

cold, and a short wool or linen tunic was worn on top. A woolen or fur shawl was worn over the shoulders and conical hats were common. Shoes were made of leather wrapped around the foot and bound by interlaced straps. Most Europeans were dressed like today's Benedictine monks, except for men's trousers. Colors were gray, brown, dark blue, and red.

Nevertheless, the people who dressed this way were representatives of the wide social structure that was the foundation of what is called the feudal pyramid, where the pope and the emperor stood at the top. Between the base and the highest point of the pyramid was a whole range of people, each tied to his or her superior and inferior. Naturally, the higher up you got the more economically secure you were, and clothes revealed the different social levels.

However, there were very few commodities and luxuries in Europe compared with the wealthy Byzantines and Moors, something the crusaders discovered when they passed through Byzantium on their way to the lands of the infidel. The people who lived on the border with the Byzantines or the Arabs, who had gotten as far as Spain and Sicily, could obtain luxury objects and fabrics, and maybe sold them to the north, but there was not a constant well-defined flow of goods, and people who lived in present-day Belgium, for example, could well have lived their lives without ever brushing against silk. No wonder then that when a merchant arrived at a village or castle and showed off a piece of shiny silk, damask, a lightly colored veil, an embroidered tunic, or a pair of leather shoes, he offered a glimpse of a different world, a world where commodities and beautiful objects were an everyday reality.

For five hundred years Europeans lived with baited breath. Then, one day in August 955, the emperor Otto the Great stopped the Hungarians on the river Lech, west of Innsbruck, and defeated them, ending the last barbarian invasion.

The nightmare was over, fear was no longer a constant companion, and people felt as if a heavy weight had been lifted from them. And while Europe was covered by a "white veil of churches," as the monk Rudolf the Bald wrote, the Europeans suddenly had a will to live, to own beautiful things of which they had had an inkling, to wear things appropriate to the fresh air they were just beginning to breathe.

Travelers or pilgrims who went to holy places had cloaks with large hoods, knapsacks, sticks, and a felt or straw hat with a wide brim.

Hood used by judges

Short tunic held by a belt

Stockings made of cloth

One kind of stocking was the soled stocking; it was made of silk and a cork sole that was also covered in silk.

Long hair was the privilege of high-ranking men. Young men shaved, whereas old men had beards. Hats were caps or hoods.

THE LATE MIDDLE AGES

After the year 1000, Europeans started to move around and look around, at home and abroad. Cities revived, arts and crafts flourished once more, and commercial traffic started to flow by land and sea. Links with the richer and more sophisticated east were strengthened by war; the Crusades were an important force in the development of Europe, which started to produce quality goods appreciated even by the sophisticated Arabs and Byzantines.

New well-to-do classes emerged in the city, where social life increased the desire to dress well, and luxury became so common that the Church felt the need to remind people of the virtues of humility.

Everyday wear for men and women consisted of a white linen tunic shirt with tight long sleeves. On top, worn as a robe, was another tunic, called a gonelle, which hung to the ground for women and was calf-length for men, often decorated with embroidery, braids, and sometimes colored cloth panels. The tunic was draped at the waist or at the hips with a belt, which was also preferably embroidered. At this time embroidery developed; it adorned and enhanced the value of brilliantly colored cloths, which became irresistible to those who could afford them.

Under the tunic men wore leggings or knee-length breeches with short socks or boots.

Over all they wore a rectangular or circular cloak. Women veiled their heads with a corner of it.

Furs were very precious and a sign of great and exclusive privilege reserved for the well-to-do classes. The richest people allowed themselves sable (wearing ermine was a king's privilege) or vair, with which they lined vermilion (a precious red or scarlet material), serge, or cloth cloaks. They also made hats, cuffs, collars, and even shoes with vair.

The oldest kind of breeches were bands of leather or cloth wound around the legs; the most recent were made of cloth. Ordinary people wore rough wool, and rich people wore linen and silk.

Clothes were decorated with frills, colorful borders, and embroidery. Women also wore light embroidered silk shoes.

Perfumes were so popular that people even sprinkled some on necklaces, and makeup was used a lot, especially by musicians, minstrels, and dancers to make them look even happier.

This young boy is wearing breeches bound at the knee with a strap, soft and certainly expensive boots, and a handkerchief on his head.

It was at this time that pearls, emeralds, sapphires, rubies, and diamonds began to be imported from the east. Necklaces, clasps, buckles, earrings, and most of all rings were made from them.

The most common colors for cloaks were green, red, and blue. The cloaks always had belts made of leather or jeweled cloth, which became very long and were knotted in front and then allowed to fall to the feet. Gloves were also very common.

Under the brightly colored hats, and especially under hoods, men often wore a cap. They also wore a short tippet, often with a hood.

Garments became longer, and men started to wear longer tunics, first used by kings and priests. The supertunic became more important than the cloak; it was made of linen or embroidered silk, colorful, and decorated with colorful borders.

Falconry was a popular pastime among the aristocracy in this era. At such events the lord took part with a large entourage.

The supertunic became longer until it had a train, and it was common practice to hold up one corner of it to show the contrast in color with the tunic underneath. Unmarried women wore their hair down or in braids and did not wear hats.

Clothes became tighter fitting thanks to buttons. A dress for a social occasion could be close fitting without the use of a belt.

Married women wore a round headdress with a wimple.

Wide hooded cloaks, with or without sleeves, were very common.

Short tunics with small cloaks and hoods and close-fitting breeches were clothes to work in.

Women at home wore only a tunic with a belt; when they went out they put on a supertunic and a cloak.

These low-heeled soft leather boots were very common and had been in use for a long time.

Points on shoes started to grow longer, until they were so excessive that it was hard to walk in them.

The most elegant shoes were a kind of embroidered cloth slipper that was protected by wearing other shoes over it. Soled stockings were still very common.

The term solers indicated the refined leather from Córdoba, recently introduced. At this time wooden or cork clogs also appeared, used especially for traveling or in bad weather.

THE THIRTEENTH AND FOURTEENTH CENTURIES

In the thirteenth and fourteenth centuries, the quality of life was steadily improving. New features like long, wide sleeves, muslin, silk interwoven with gold, and veils arrived from the east. People started to wear fustian and velvet, and western decoration like square shapes, circles, polka dots, and butterfly designs appeared.

Rich men wore a shirt and tight cloth breeches, a short tunic that was tight over the chest and then flared from the waist down, and a woolen, linen, or heavy silk robe, embroidered, decorated, and fixed at the waist with a leather belt. Over this, they wore a cloak either open at the front or closed and pulled over the head and often lined with fur.

Women wore a linen or silk shirt and cloth leggings as underwear, a long tunic that was tight over the chest and flared from the waist down, and a robe with detachable sleeves that trailed to the ground. Typical accessories for men and women were bags that were attached to the belt with long straps and were used as pockets, which had not been invented yet.

There were many tailors' shops in the fifteenth century, thanks to the use of close-fitting garments that required skill to make. The best tailors worked in the city, and their fee was often determined by law.

This seamstress is wearing a hennin, the tall cylindrical hat with a transparent veil typical of this period.

THE MERCHANTS AND TAILORS OF THE 1400S

In the 1400s the textile industry and commerce experienced a time of prosperity. Production of embroidered fabrics reached a very high technical and artistic standard, especially in Italy, favored by the commercial relations established by the Crusades. Milan was famous for its velvet, and there was a demand for Italian silks and fustian. In the early part of the century, Venice began to produce extraordinary brocaded velvet, with designs sometimes drawn by famous painters like Antonio Pollaiuolo. In Florence in 1472 there were a good 270 woolen drapers' shops, and the export of heavy camlet and light serge was lucrative.

The Italian cities, however, had competition from Paris, Poitiers, Rheims, Tours, and Lyons in France and Almería, Granada, and Seville in Spain.

As for the manufacturers, tailors were mostly men, because women's dresses were usually made at home. Tailors took pride in their ability to cut fabric, so much so that their corporate symbol was a pair of scissors. But apart from tailors and fabric producers, the fashion sector incorporated a diverse range of specialist artisans including jewelers, furriers, perfumers, cobblers, cap makers, knitters, dyers, and so on. Then there were the haberdashers, with shops/bazaars where one could find fabrics, ready-made clothes, yarns, and every kind of accessory from bags to belts, masks, spurs, knives, and naturally needles, scissors, and a number of other tools necessary for creating what had now become very complicated clothes.

Across Europe, the commercial centers that maintained links with the east experienced a surge. Among the most important were Venice, Florence, Ghent, and Bruges, but there were many others.

THE END OF THE MIDDLE AGES

In the 1400s Europe's attitude to life changed, and people began to pay less attention to the supernatural and concentrated on the individual. Feudalism was coming to an end, while manufacturing and commerce created new economically powerful social groups. Luxury increased in the courts and cities, where the new bourgeoisie wanted clothes to show that they could compete with castle noblemen.

Fashion varied from one region to another. In the mid-1300s, the long flowing robe had been abandoned by both men and women in favor of short cloaks for men and long, tight gowns for women. Men's tunics were replaced by a short doublet or waistcoat, which was tight and padded. Breeches had various shapes: they were tight in Italy and wide and crossed with vertical slashes in central Europe. Sleeves changed too; they were now decorated with trimmings or fur and had similar vertical slashes through which a white shirt was visible underneath. The practice of slashing clothes started in Germany and then spread elsewhere.

Women's clothes became tight over the top half of the body, while the long train slimmed the figure. Girdles were constantly becoming tighter and necklines lower, even though they were sometimes covered by a light veil. Attached to the bodice were the skirt, with soft folds, and the sleeves, which were very long and very precious.

Rich fabrics like damask, taffeta, and every kind of silk were preferred, and accessories like gloves, hats, and bags were popular.

Low necklines were covered (but not always!) by chemisettes or veils. Hair was held up by gold nets encrusted with precious gems. Usually the aristocracy preferred dark colors, whereas ordinary people showed off in brightly colored materials.

In Germany belts, shoes, hems, and necklines were commonly decorated with bells, and garments were slashed so the chemise could puff out from underneath.

These pages picture German fashions.

Men had short hair and shaved their faces or wore short beards.

Women had very long hair put up in different ways.

The simple precision of Renaissance architecture is an appropriate backdrop for sixteenth-century society, where splendor and austerity, internal searching and the desire to display oneself, great vanities and great culture, lived side by side.

SOCIETY IN THE 1500S

Lucretia Borgia, one of the most elegant women of the sixteenth century, had fifty gowns, many of which were embroidered in gold, and eighty-six pairs of shoes, which were also very ornate. In fact, shoes were so expensive that intellectuals, and probably husbands too, were often denouncing them, saying, "Women should have been created without feet."

It is true that in the 1500s, because of the healthy economy, luxury increased excessively and became the favorite way of showing off prestige and power among the upper classes. For this reason sumptuary laws were introduced, but even then the legislators were noblemen, so the laws focused on the rich middle classes that competed with them. In Venice, for example, only the doge and his family were allowed luxury, but there were many exceptions for nobles, who could wear particular gold and silver fabrics when the king visited them. This is why King Henry III of France, when visiting Venice in 1574, was amazed when he saw noblewomen's attire at the celebrations held in his honor: "The decorations on hats, bosoms, and at the neck of pearls, jewels set in gold, were judged to be of a value of 500,000 scudi for each lady, and collars, corsets, and sleeves were all covered in jewels, pearls, and gold."

But ornament was not the only way to display power. Another way, which had always been common but was typical of this century, was trying to appear majestic by increasing one's height or the space occupied by one's body. Noblewomen must have seemed really regal when they wore the vertingale, which stiffened and widened the skirt, and a steel busk that fell in a point in front of the bodice and was so dangerous and painful that it was prohibited. The gown was just as impressive, a wide, stiff cloak with sleeves that were so wide that they gave the wearer no less than a haughty air. The gown perfectly expressed the desire of the nobility to stand out, completely in contrast to the thoughtfulness of previous centuries.

People suffered trying to look splendid, and sometimes they just ended up looking ridiculous. In one of his comedies, the poet

Kings

Pope

High aristocracy

Merchants and bankers

City bourgeois, craftsmen, clerics, and artists

Peasants, laborers, and servants

Ludovico Ariosto made fun of such nobles who "widen their shoulders with felt and paste-board and whose crane-like legs become Herculean with cotton-wool and rags."

However, in the 1500s garments did not always mean extravagance, luxury, or eccentricity; there were activities and roles with precise uniforms. The color of one's cloak could signify a profession or social status: in Venice doctors and ministers wore a purple robe, and generals wore turquoise; merchants wore shorter cloaks; and ordinary people settled for brown. As well as cloaks, gowns could have different colors depending on the wearer's profession. Scholars liked red, lawyers and theologians wore black, and students wore dark colors. Don't forget that apart from frills and decorations, this was a century of great cultural activity facilitated by the invention of the printing press. So along with nobles and rich bourgeois in the contest for appearance, there were also intellectuals, who in their study wore austere and comfortable church apparel. When Niccolò Machiavelli wrote his historical/political works, he would wear a toga, because this symbol of the Roman Republic inspired him.

THE SIXTEENTH CENTURY

In the sixteenth century the taste for elegance and pleasure was greater than ever and became even more ornate. Very rich materials like heavy cloth fabrics, embroidery, precious jewels, and laces were used, while from newly discovered America fashion acquired gold and silver, exotic birds' feathers for hats and fans, lapis lazuli, jades, pearls, and mother-of-pearl.

Thanks to printing, the first fashion magazines appeared spreading news, and ladies exchanged dolls dressed up in the latest fashions. People also started to study good manners. *The Courtier* by Baldassare Castiglione and *The Galateo* by Giovanni della Casa became popular throughout Europe along with Italian fashion, which set the rules.

Women's clothes consisted of a tight bodice stiffened with whalebones, an underskirt, and a rich skirt over that. Necklines were very low, and sleeves were detachable. Embroidery was very popular, especially in Venice. The chemise became very important; it was white and decorated in gold or black, a very popular color; and people even slept in it. Under the skirt women wore breeches and silk or woolen stockings.

Men's apparel consisted of a chemise, a doublet that was heavily decorated in front and on the sleeves, which were ever wider and puffier and sometimes slashed as in Germany, breeches or skirts that were knee-length or just below the knee, stockings, and cloaks of various shapes.

Shoes had a wide sole and a rounded tip and were often very decorative.

As usual, jewelry was especially popular, particularly heavy gold chains. Gloves and bags were also very popular decorative accessories, and it was compulsory to keep a new invention called a pocket watch.

People also used large quantities of perfumes like civet, amber, and musk; and they doused hats, gloves, saddles, stockings, and shoes with perfume. The more they used the less they washed.

In England Tudor hats were popular (left), made of a frame of precious material which was attached to a cap.

The ruff collar rising behind the head was very popular, but heels that were half a meter high and made it difficult for women to move without support did not last.

The face was emphasized by hairstyles that left the forehead clear.

Hair was brushed back or gathered in precious hair nets, hats, or stiff linen or silk hats from which hung veils.

Even men liked low square necklines that showed the chemise at the top. Belts were metal, often gold or silver, but also cloth, knotted and left to fall in front.

Cassocks that fell to the feet were worn by the upper classes, especially in Venice. Furs were still very popular, and hats were decorated with ostrich feathers. German trunk hose became fashionable.

Spanish fashion   Dutch fashion

THE EARLY 1600S

European fashion in the second half of the 1500s and in the first half of the 1600s was mainly Spanish and reflected the climate of the Counter Reformation, that is, the more disciplined aspect of the Catholic Church after the Protestant Reformation. It was a severe fashion, uncomfortable and somber. The high ruff impeded natural movements of the head and made it hard to smile normally, giving an air of haughtiness. A person's needs were completely sacrificed in favor of an image.

Men wore a chemise with a ruff, a padded doublet, padded short breeches, stockings, and ornate shoes. On top they wore a short, wide cloak of stiff silk, which was mainly decorative.

Women too wore a stiff bodice, a ruff that meant hair had to be put up, and long petticoats with an overskirt that was wider at the bottom. Petticoats were held and stiffened by vertingales, iron hoops with whalebones for noble and rich women.

In the early 1600s there was another kind of fashion in the Netherlands, the richest country of that time. It was the opposite of Spanish style in that it gave men longer, looser doublets with less noticeable padding, a higher waist, and wider, longer breeches that were tucked into turned-up funnel boots.

Men let their hair grow long and started to use large felt hats with feathers, originally a peasant practice.

Women didn't like busking or padding; they wore higher waists than the Spanish and from rigid ruffs they moved on to falling collars that adorned low necklines, which had begun to reappear.

Soon all clothing became lighter. Sleeves became shorter, skirts were looser, while fashionable jewels became discreet strings of pearls.

The seventeenth century's passion for attaching lace to everything started in the Netherlands. The Dutch put lace on collars, shoulders, cuffs, and shoes. Most important of all were handkerchiefs and gloves.

Winter dress involved the use of fur, especially in the north, and large shawls.

Peasants' clothes were clearly simple and practical. Women covered their head with veils and wore long sleeves and aprons. The dress bodice was often detached from the skirt for comfort.

Boots were abandoned in favor of silk stockings, so that King Louis XIV could show off his perfect legs.

THE STYLE OF THE SUN KING

In 1643 Louis XIV was crowned king of France, known as the Sun King, and at his court in Versailles he imposed a fashion that was actively spread throughout Europe and America by way of waist-high dressed dolls and, from 1672, by a newspaper called *Le Mercure Galant*. Adopted everywhere, French fashion brought together the different dress of the dominant European classes, though allowing regional variations. It was in this age that wigs first appeared, destined to become a very important French feature. The success of this accessory, exclusive to the aristocracy, was due also to the majesty that it gave the wearer.

Aside from the five thousand people who worked in the king's service, five thousand members of the aristocracy lived in Versailles who had been forced to stay there so that the king could control them politically. He controlled them through clothes as well, which were very elaborate and very expensive.

During the first half of the Sun King's reign, which lasted until 1715, clothes were

From ruffs, to large lace collars, to variously shaped collars. By the end of the century the cravat, the ancestor of the tie, was introduced. It was part of the military uniform of Croatian mercenaries, present in all the armies of the day, and civilians liked the cravat so much that they adopted it.

quite light and allowed a certain amount of freedom, but they became ever more extravagant and splendid.

Men's fashions changed many times, but a long tight garment remained popular; it was open at the front and worn with very large breeches called rhinegraves, tied above the knee with frills, lace, and ribbons, similar to short skirts. There was elaborate embroidery everywhere, on chemises and bodices, on breeches, shoes, and gloves.

Even women were elegant but not as extravagant as men; the bodice neckline was lowered to expose the shoulders and was adorned with a flat collar. The two traditional skirts now had a third skirt, open at the front and folded, or puffed at the sides by knotted ribbons, clasps, and pins.

Stockings were of silk, usually white or flesh-colored for women. Men's shoes had a square point and were made of silk or velvet, black or of the same color as the clothes, embroidered and encrusted with jewels. Women's shoes had the same shape but were usually of the same material as their dress.

It became fashionable for men to have long hair. At this time men were more frivolous than women; sometimes they wore as many as three hundred bows on a single garment.

Louis XIV promoted the use of heels to hide how short he was.

While Spanish fashion was still devoted to dark colors, the French preferred light colors with very strange names. Who knows what these colors were: "mortal sin," "desire for love," and "dying Spaniard"?

In the 1600s children's clothes had started to become simpler, but they were still replicas of adult clothes.

The cravat established itself and was usually a strip of lace or linen embroidered with lace around the neck. As in the past furs were still cherished even in the form of muffs.

A typical hairstyle was a commode, a starched linen headdress with folded piping.

Stockings were made of red, pink, light blue, and yellow silk, and shoes had high heels or were open, decorated with buckles, rosettes, or diamonds. One accessory for men that no member of the aristocracy ever forgot was the sword. This habit of walking around armed caused many duels.

Men's long hair meant that, since not everyone had the right curls, they had to rely on wigs a lot more, and later these became generally used.

THE EARLY 1700S

Toward the end of the seventeenth century, garments became less extravagant but more ornate. In this period three fundamental pieces of clothing still in use today were introduced: the jacket, the waistcoat, and trousers.

The jacket, which was usually brocaded and colorful, was lengthened to just below the knee and took on a frock-coat shape, tight at the waist and wider at the bottom with a split at the back; sleeves were tighter and decorated with large braids around the wrists.

The waistcoat, launched at the end of the 1600s by Giles, a character in French comedy, was as long as the jacket and had many buttons and low pockets.

There were tight knee-length trousers, called culottes.

Silk shirts decorated with lace appeared from under the jacket and were very popular.

Women wore close-fitting bodices reinforced with whalebones, very low necklines, and sleeves that were decorated with cascades of lace below the elbow. The petticoat, not too wide but richly decorated, was sewn to the bodice. The gown, which was also very ornate and of a different color from the petticoat, was made of satin or velvet.

Society clothing was very elaborate and dressing was not an easy matter, but by the middle of the century a French actress called Adrienne launched a garment for traveling and relaxing at home which was comfortable and baggy, called an adrienne or a negligee. This garment spread throughout Europe too, because French fashion was still in the lead, so much so that during the reign of Louis XIV, a corporation of dressmakers was formed, which took over female fashion, bringing in new ideas.

The 1700s were the years of elegant accessories: small soft-colored umbrellas and parasols, feather, lace, or silk fans, and naturally many jewels, with a preference for diamonds.

Both sexes had poor hygiene and masked bad smells with large doses of perfume and by changing their underwear frequently. Cologne water, perfected in Germany by the Italian Farina brothers, was popular probably for this reason.

GETTING DRESSED IS SUCH A BOTHER!

Typical of this century was the wide petticoat, which appeared in 1718 and triumphed for almost seventy years. It was held up by a pannier. At first this was a skirt where three ever-decreasing hoops moved toward the waist, with a fourth hoop that was waist size. Later only the metallic structure remained, whose hoops changed shape until they became elliptical. Women used large panniers, if not enormous ones, in society, and smaller ones at home. Panniers, however, were very uncomfortable, which is why the negligee was greeted with such relief in midcentury.

On top of the pannier was the petticoat, which was made of precious materials and decorated with lace, bows, and artificial flowers. The robe on top remained open to show the delicacy of the petticoat underneath.

The taste for extravagance was obvious in every piece of clothing: wigs, which were always white, became so high that they brushed against chandeliers, sometimes catching fire.

A cushion on which the woman could rest her arms was tied over each hip; otherwise she'd have to hold her arms out straight.

The purpose of the hoops was to create a marked contrast between the wide skirts and the delicate, narrow waist and chest. For this reason, the waist was ferociously squeezed tight with laces and then fastened with a metal belt.

Delicate high-heeled shoes were made of silk for people who didn't walk a lot.

The size of these dresses inhibited movement and even led to changes in furniture, since, for example, women could sit only on armless benches. Because of the popularity of wigs, real hair was not important until the reign of Marie Antoinette, the unfortunate queen of France. She had beautiful blond hair, so she decided to end the reign of wigs, and from that moment on real hair became important again.

THE FRENCH REVOLUTION

While nobles were dressing in ever more exaggerated ways, the middle classes continued to develop their own style, which ultimately prevailed. Toward 1785 heavy embroidery and bright colors were disappearing, and men's fabrics were leaning toward discreet pinstripes. The pannier was cast aside, fashion came in line with the rational illuminism that pervaded the age, and English styles were imitated.

In England, thanks to the love of the outdoors and the fact that many members of the aristocracy lived in the country, garments were definitely more practical. The English wore riding coats, overcoats that were ideal for horse riding, on top of a short waistcoat, simple trousers, leather shoes, and a top hat.

Far more important than the English influence, however, was the French Revolution of 1789, which imposed the middle-class style of dress. Men renounced bright colors, variety, and decoration and concentrated on practicality. English fashion was popularized, and if trousers were short at first, with time long trousers buttoned at the front, used by the sans-culottes, took over. The word *sans-culotte* was invented to indicate scornfully the lower classes, that is, people who did not wear the short culottes of the aristocracy.

After the revolution fashion remained practical, but the desire for elegance and variety revived, though limited now to women's clothes. This is how Grecian dress came about, in the form of shapeless shifts—nightshirts made of light materials like linen, cambric, and voile and with low necklines that emphasized the bosom—as well as the more formal coureur, made of a short jacket, tight bodice, waistcoat, and hat with the republican cockade.

Typical French clothing

Grecian-style dress

A coureur

Hair color became natural again. There were different kinds of hats.

This typical sans-culotte wears a bicorne hat with cockade, waistcoat, chemise with bow, jacket with pockets, and long trousers. He is wearing clogs on his feet.

Low leather shoes became popular, as did soft turnover boots.

THE EARLY 1800S

The French Revolution had confirmed the authority of the bourgeoisie, and clothing was simplified to adapt to a society of entrepreneurs, professionals, and workers. However, when Napoleon proclaimed himself emperor in 1804, he set out to revive the splendor of Versailles and called Leroy to his court, a favorite tailor of the aristocracy and now of the revolutionaries, who became the authority on style. Imperial dress was born.

Trimmings, laces, and flounces returned to women's clothes, while men turned once more to short, tight, knee-length culottes, and embroidery graced military uniforms once more.

Napoleon wanted not just a magnificent court, but also a successful textile industry, and he used fashion and its whims to make expensive fabrics produced in Italian and French factories (crepe, cashmere, satin, taffeta, and velvet) obligatory.

Women's garments were designed with a high waist just under the bosom and had very low round or square necklines. Hems were decorated with light ruffs and gold embroidery. Sleeves had many different shapes;

The cravat became a very important accessory, and there were many ways of tying it. The English were particularly imaginative at this.

The imperial style did not have much influence abroad and did not make any great changes to the fashion of the bourgeoisie, which adopted it only on ceremonial occasions.

The lower classes were even less influenced by the new fashion. This boy is wearing wooden clogs filled with straw, which were used by the lower classes in the winter as protection against bad weather.

some were very short and worn with long gloves that covered the arm, others were long or had puffs down to the wrist. The seam between the skirt and the short bodice was hidden by trimmings, fringes, or embroidered belts clasped with pins, and the skirt was decorated with large folds gathered at the back and ending in a short train. To keep such lightly dressed women warm, cashmere shawls became fashionable, the first of which was given to Josephine by Napoleon.

Men continued to imitate English style; trousers were slowly beginning to resemble those of today, and the short jacket continued to be worn, either as a frock coat or a tailcoat, while ornaments were limited to collars and ties.

Man's leather shoe

Woman's cloth shoe

Woman's leather slipper

Wooden clog used by peasants and the lower classes

THE NINETEENTH CENTURY

The nineteenth century was not a very inventive time for fashion. After Napoleon, waists went back to the usual place in women's garments, and the corset reappeared. The skirt became conical and started to widen, brightened by sewn-on decorations or printed fabrics with vivid patterns. Sleeves became very large and had padded puffs. Shawls were still used. Hairstyles became tidier, as braids gathered in a bun or with bunches of curls pulled behind the ear.

Toward the middle of the century luxurious clothes were again popular, and for the third time in history large rigid skirts appeared. In the 1800s, this kind of skirt was called a crinoline, because of the padded material that was used to make the stiff supporting underskirt, replaced later with a metal net of rings and horseshoes. The crinoline required enormous quantities of cloth, especially when flounces became fashionable, and expensive materials like silk, satin, taffeta, brocade, and in the summer crepe, tulle, and muslin were favored. Elegance was therefore quite costly.

Jackets could be buttoned at the chest or only at the waist. In any case, men liked to have a slender waist as much as women did and tied wide sashes around it.

A woman would not leave the house without a hat.

Shawls of all kinds never lost favor with women.

Even this fashion was uncomfortable, but fortunately women wore negligees at home.

Men's fashion, by contrast, continued to simplify in ties, hairstyles, three-quarter-length coats, and low shoes. Romantics tended to prefer black, but they also wore blue or brown tailcoats, and the more imaginative gentleman could do what he liked with his waistcoat. In midcentury tails became evening wear and trousers widened a little. The cane became an indispensable accessory.

Thus fashion was determined by two factors that became more and more important: the increase in the number of people with secure financial status and industry, which produced textiles and other accessories at low cost, at the same time creating a new group of customers—the lower-middle-class worker.

At the beginning of the century shops appeared with ready-made dresses of various prices: Quenin in Paris, Korn and Hostrupp in Hamburg. Not long after, the American Isaac Singer produced a sewing machine, and dressing decoratively was no longer a luxury reserved for the privileged few.

Cloaks originally meant for soldiers became common, and in order to tie the cravat—which was usually white or black—with comfort, men adopted shirts with high collars.

The number of skirts a woman could wear increased to seven, all of different materials.

With the introduction of crinoline, small waists became fashionable again, and the corset reinforced with whalebone or steel became a real torture.

Politician	Nurse	Grenadier	Fireman	Postman	Naval officer
Jockey	Railman	Milliner	Doctor	Judge	Miner
Peasant	Coachman	Working woman	Ballerina	Cowboy	Soldier

NINETEENTH-CENTURY SOCIETY

After 1820 neoclassical style was abandoned and ladies started to wear ostrich feathers and large artificial flowers in their hair which were so big that their hairdos were larger than their umbrellas.

Skirts widened and stiffened again, sleeves widened until they became excessive. In short, ostentatious dressing was back in fashion to distinguish individuals who belonged to the privileged classes.

Compared with the previous century, however, dress was not that ostentatious because the middle-class capitalists and industrialists did not indulge in oddities, and the wealthy concentrated on following fashions accurately. When romantic colors like "fainting rose," "suppressed sigh," or "dust of ancient ruins" appeared, women quickly adopted them. The

aristocracy and upper middle class, however, were quickly copied by the middle class, so that the desire to distinguish oneself led people to change clothes yet again. And since fashion magazines spread new styles very quickly, the changes occurred at a fast pace.

The veiled hat became popular, lending the wearer an air of mystery, as well as silk underwear with its unmistakable rustle, gloves without which men and women could not go out, and canes and hats, indispensable for fashionable men.

The strange history of the overcoat begins around 1838. Gabriel d'Orsay, known as the most elegant man in Europe, was caught in a downpour and to keep from getting soaked bought a paletot from a sailor, which was a rough popular jacket. Soon after, there was a scandal in the fashion magazines, and the garment was adopted by dandies, the elegant men who determined what was fashionable.

The 1800s were the years of romanticism, and stylish women had to look pale and languid. For this they used parasols and gloves to keep them from getting a tan like peasant women. Men, on the other hand, had a romantic air if their hairstyle looked natural, as if it were tossed by a stormy wind, like Lord Byron's.

Children wore the aristocratic uniform of Eton College—a short jacket and long trousers—and later were dressed in sailors' uniforms.

In this century different clothes became typical of different professions, and sometimes became actual uniforms. New for the time was the rail worker's uniform: a blue jacket and flat peaked cap. Bakers and milkmen normally wore white clothes and caps, and bricklayers and house painters wore pointed hats made of newspaper.

In rich people's houses cooks wore a white jacket and cap, maids wore little white aprons, and butlers wore a pinstriped suit in which to clean and on special evenings splendid liveries calculated to emphasize the family's power. These expensive liveries were eventually replaced by dark tailcoats with golden cords and crested buttons on important occasions, and a tailcoat, waistcoat, black tie, and white gloves for everyday wear. Coachmen wore a top hat, a green tailcoat with gold buttons, and lightly colored trousers tucked into turnover boots.

Prisoners were instantly recognizable by their yellow clothes. Highwaymen wore pointed hats decorated with ribbons, coats covered in chevrons, gold chains, a cloak, and, of course, carried a blunderbuss, which, even without the ribbons, pointed hat, and so on, was enough to identify them.

Another garment served to identify the so-called yellow-glove thieves, refined criminals who wore gloves identical to those worn by gentlemen, which was only natural since the thieves themselves were gentlemen.

Romantic artists of this century wore a beret; the soft berets worn by painters, which were usually tipped to one side, were considered "Raphaelesque."

Elegant evening wear was always matched by high-heeled shoes.

City clothes could be bought ready-made. Parasols and fans were still fashionable.

A wintry version of the chesterfield coat could have fur trimmings.

TOWARD THE NEW CENTURY

Like the aristocracy they replaced at the top of the social scale, the bourgeois were careful to adjust their way of life to their new role. So they spent quite a lot of money building appropriate houses and decorating them, surrounding themselves with servants, and on clothing.

The old aristocracy had lost its absolute power but still had the prestige of its name, and many descendants of famous lineages had with time transformed themselves into capitalists similar to the bourgeoisie that had toppled them.

In addition to these elite groups, a vast social mix of people were steadily working toward comfort, although with difficulty, and modeling themselves on the life of the rich middle class, who were still quite often big employers.

Toward the end of the century there were many fashions and a lot of confusion about style, because society was varied and needs were so many. The crinoline, however, was replaced by just one petticoat and a horizontal tight-fitting skirt called a bustle that lifted the back of the skirt, so that it gave a very

There were various hairstyles, often pulled up at the back with a bow. There were also many different hats.

unnatural shape, whereas the corset was tight on the chest to accentuate the bosom.

Cities favored simplicity, thanks to shops stocked with ready-made clothes. Jackets were a bit masculine and fabrics simple, with a leather belt, the bodice like a chemise with a high collar; each garment competed to respond to the practical needs of women, who had started to lead a more active life.

Vanity had its revenge when it came to evening wear: soft silhouettes, low necklines, trains. When skirts got shorter, heels got higher.

For men, jackets and tailcoats remained the most important garments; the frock coat or chesterfield was a popular overcoat distinguished by its hidden fastening, and the greatcoat by its tight waist. Later the dinner jacket would become evening wear.

The most popular among hats was the top hat, and the cane was still essential. The days when a king or his wife could influence fashion were over, and now fashion authorities were great tailors like Worth and Doucet, who like kings launched new styles at a heady pace.

Men's colors became more sober: black, gray, brown, blue. Men adopted a more serious look, which only a tie could soften.

A TAILOR'S SHOP IN THE EARLY 1900S

By the early 1900s ready-made clothes stores that also sold underwear had been around for a while. However, mass production began only after the invention of the sewing machine, and only then were department stores what they are today. Here you could find a bit of everything: clothes, shoes, hats, perfumes, and things like laces, toys, plates, and underwear. You could go in, look around, try this and that, and not buy anything.

Mass production in the clothing industry was not as developed as it is today, and tailors still had a lot to do; both fashion leaders and the less famous could count on a numerous clientele that still preferred clothes made to measure. In England, which had long dominated men's fashions, the best men's tailors were in London, and their shops were all gathered together in just one street, Savile Row.

One important novelty was the reappearance of seamstresses. After having founded a corporation in France during the reign of Louis XIV, they had gone back into the shadows, and tailors had dominated the field in the nineteenth century. In the new century women dressmakers were back on the scene, never to leave it again.

Tailors and dressmakers of high fashion

strenuously defended their boutiques from the assault of mass production, but eventually had to face up to economic competitiveness and change their methods; tailors' creations were reserved for clients who could afford them, and a different kind of product was destined for general consumption. Mass-produced garments became stylish and dressing well was no longer a privilege. However, good taste was and will always remain a privilege that no tailor can sell.

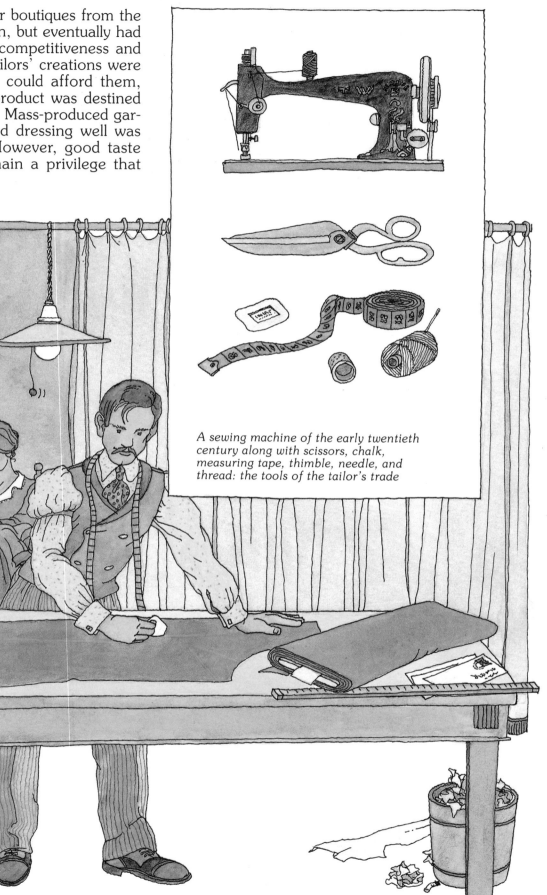

A sewing machine of the early twentieth century along with scissors, chalk, measuring tape, thimble, needle, and thread: the tools of the tailor's trade

How women dressed before the Great War

The corset, hated by doctors, emphasized the hips and bosom.

THE 1900S

While men's clothing remained unchanged, at the beginning of the twentieth century women were squeezed into corsets, wore large hats, boleros with cascades of lace, wide skirts, and bodices with pearls and fringes. Later the corset disappeared, the ladies' tailor-made was perfected, and skirts were shortened to the ankle.

But the Great War provoked radical changes; women had participated in this war even in roles usually reserved for men, and there were many women who now worked.

When the war was over, practicality and simplicity were the needs of the new lifestyle. So shorter skirts, freer necks, comfortable sleeves, and light shoes with sensible heels appeared.

Hair and hats also became simpler. Women even cut their hair, causing a great scandal; soon after they started to wear trousers, encouraged by the sporting life and cinema— a new and powerful way of transmitting fashions and lifestyles.